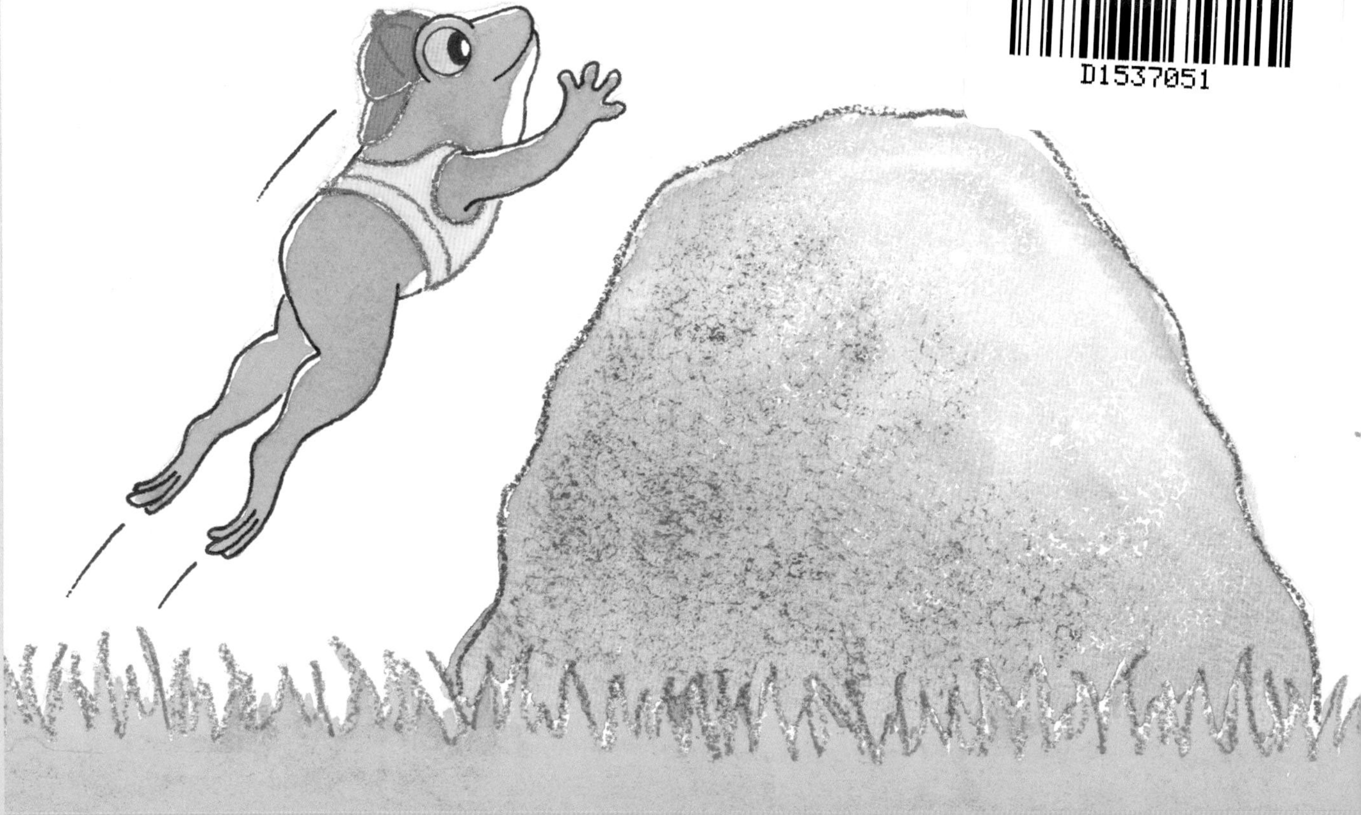

Bob hops up.

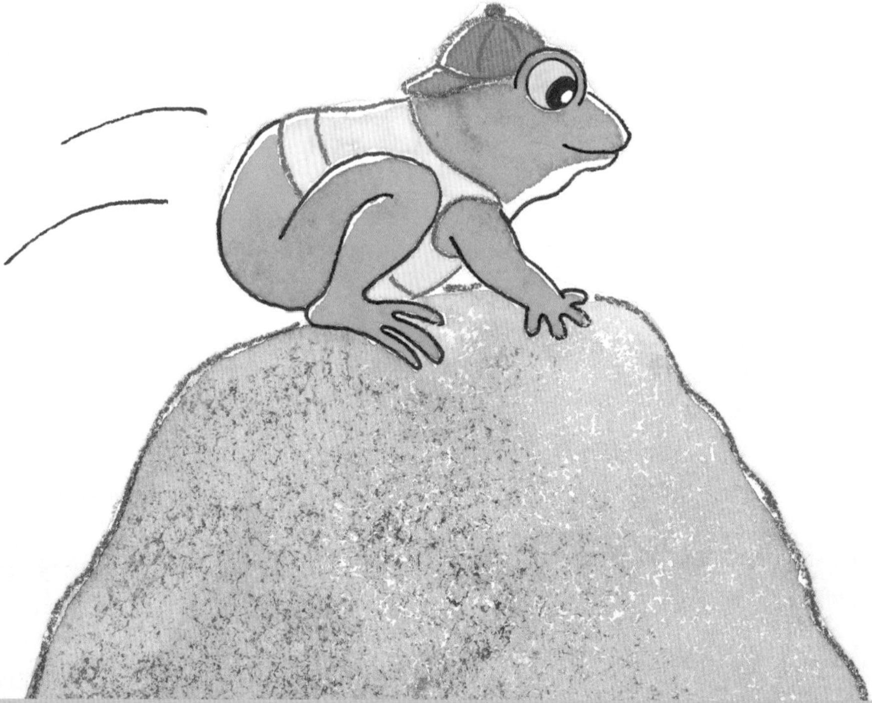

Bob lands on the rock.

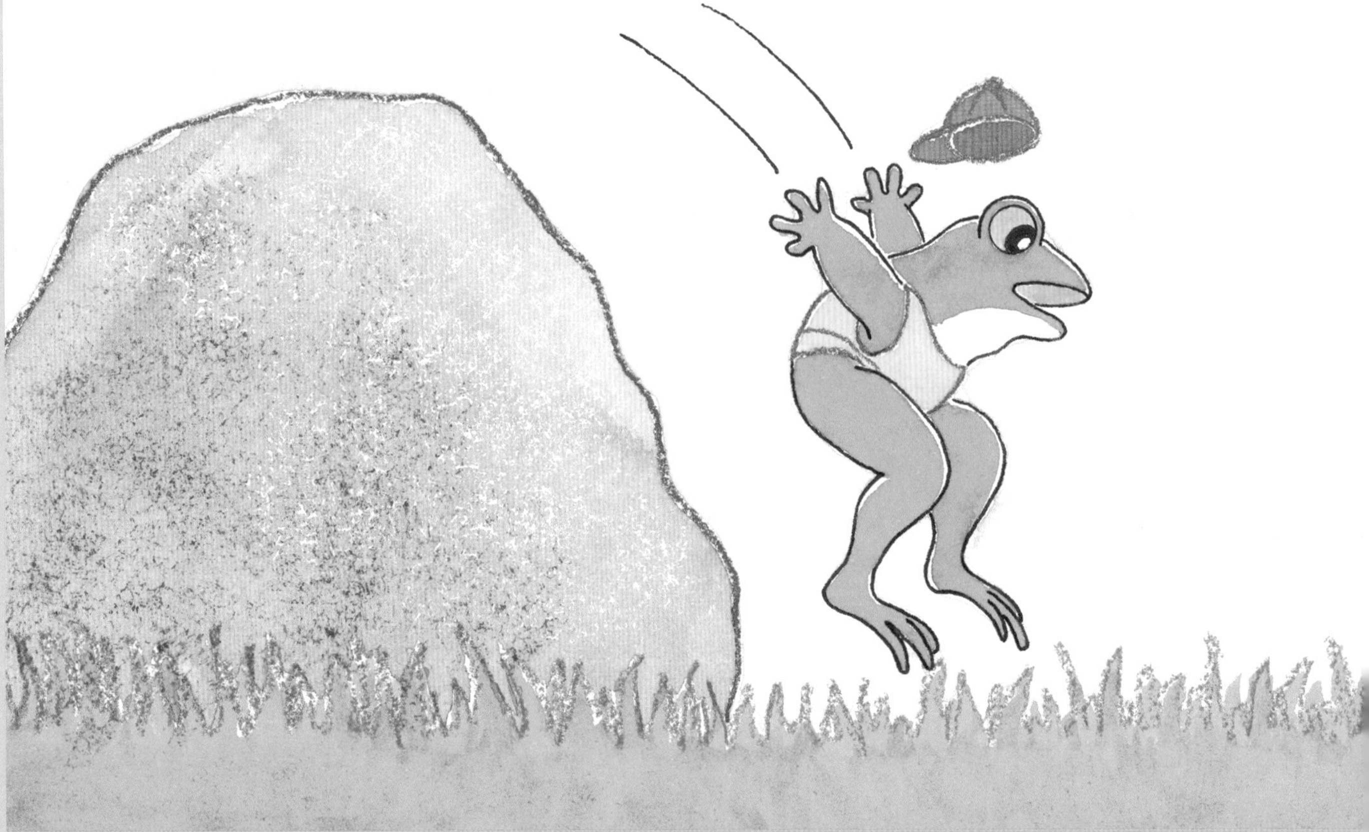

Bob hops down.

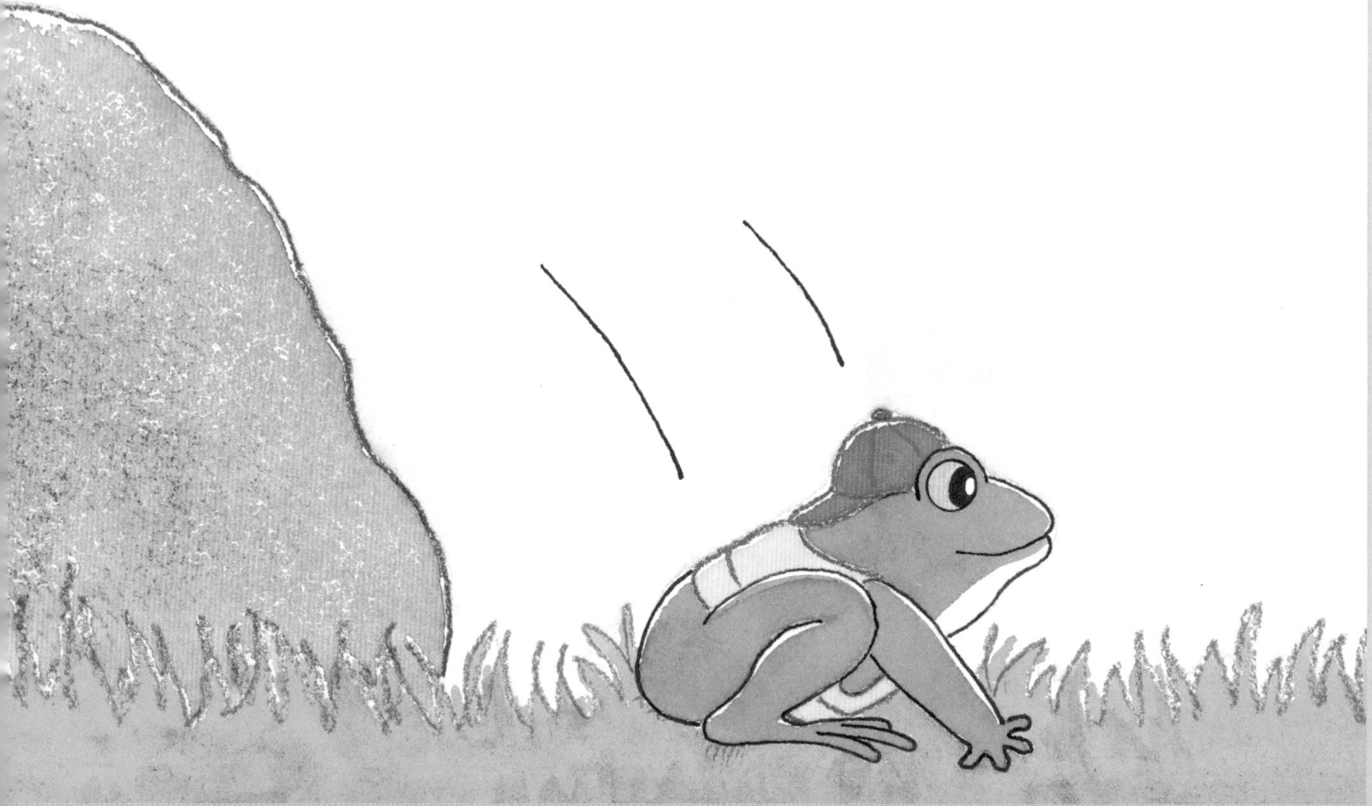

Bob lands on the grass.

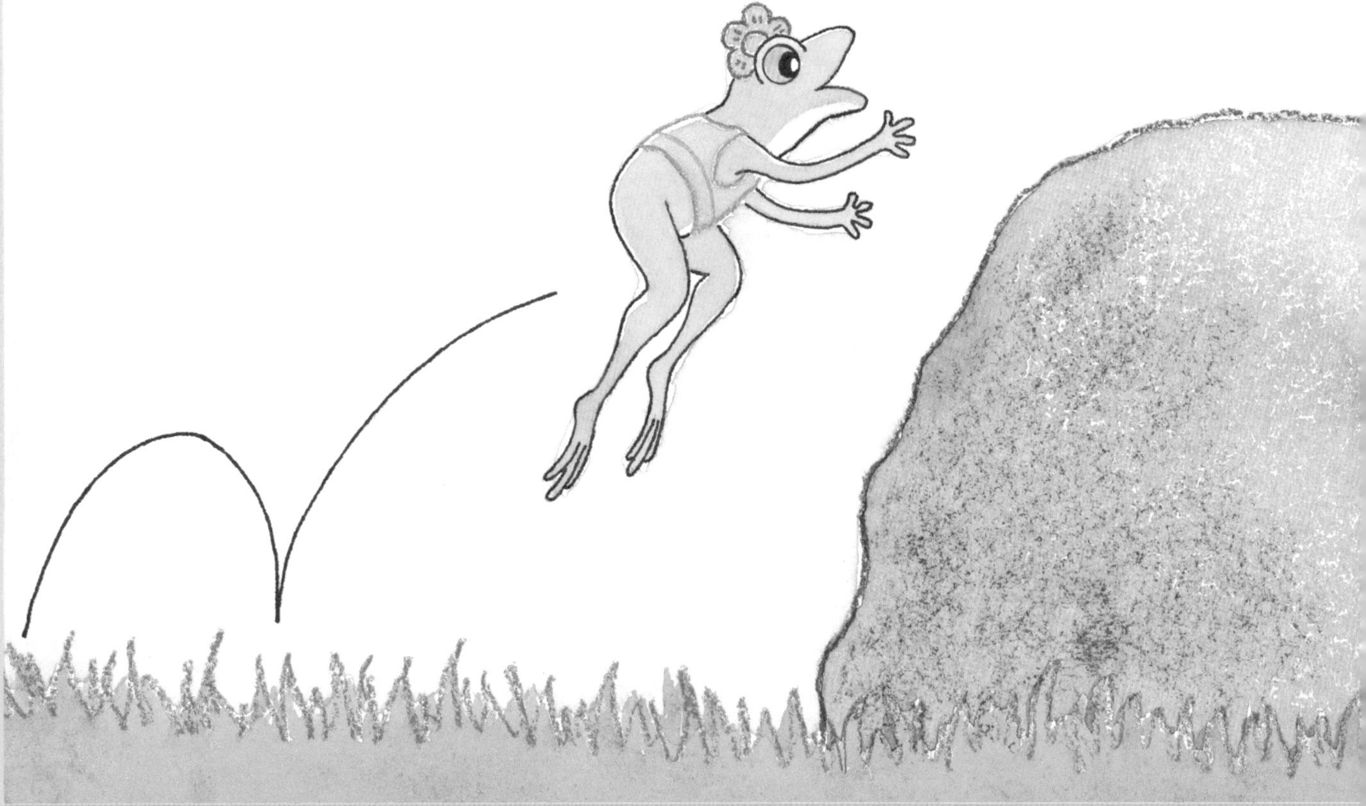

Lucy hops up.

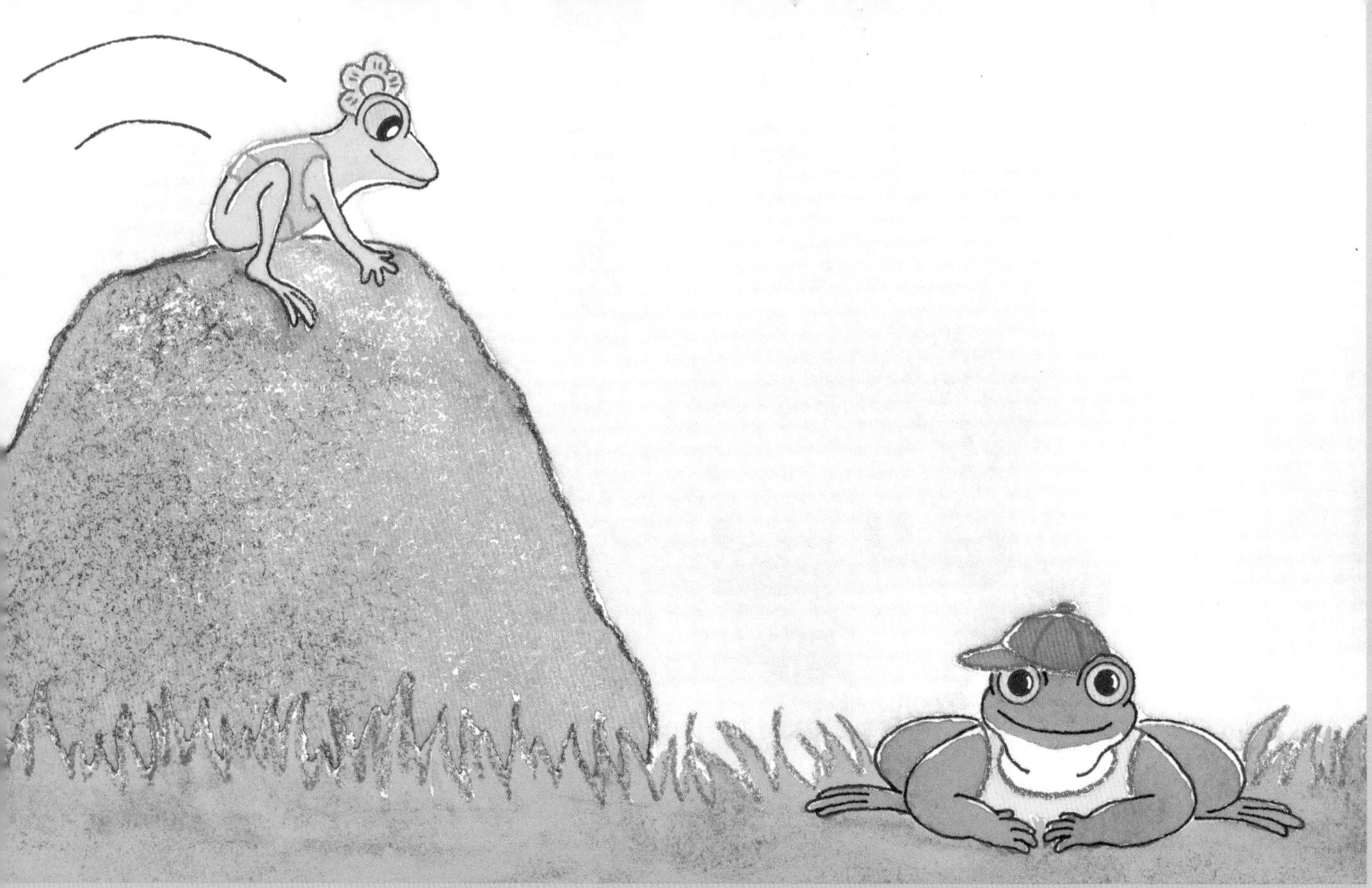

Lucy lands on the rock.

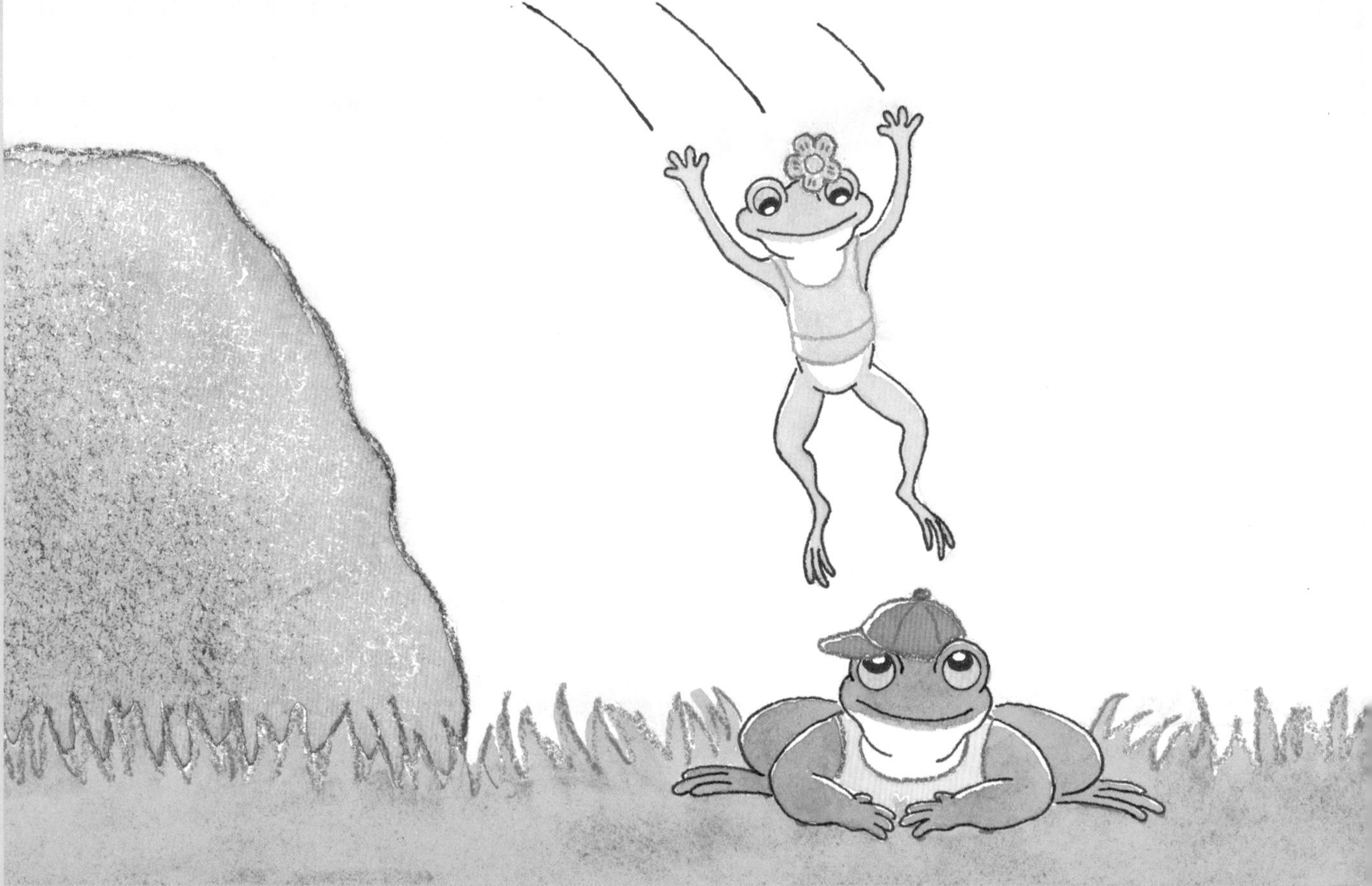

Lucy hops down.

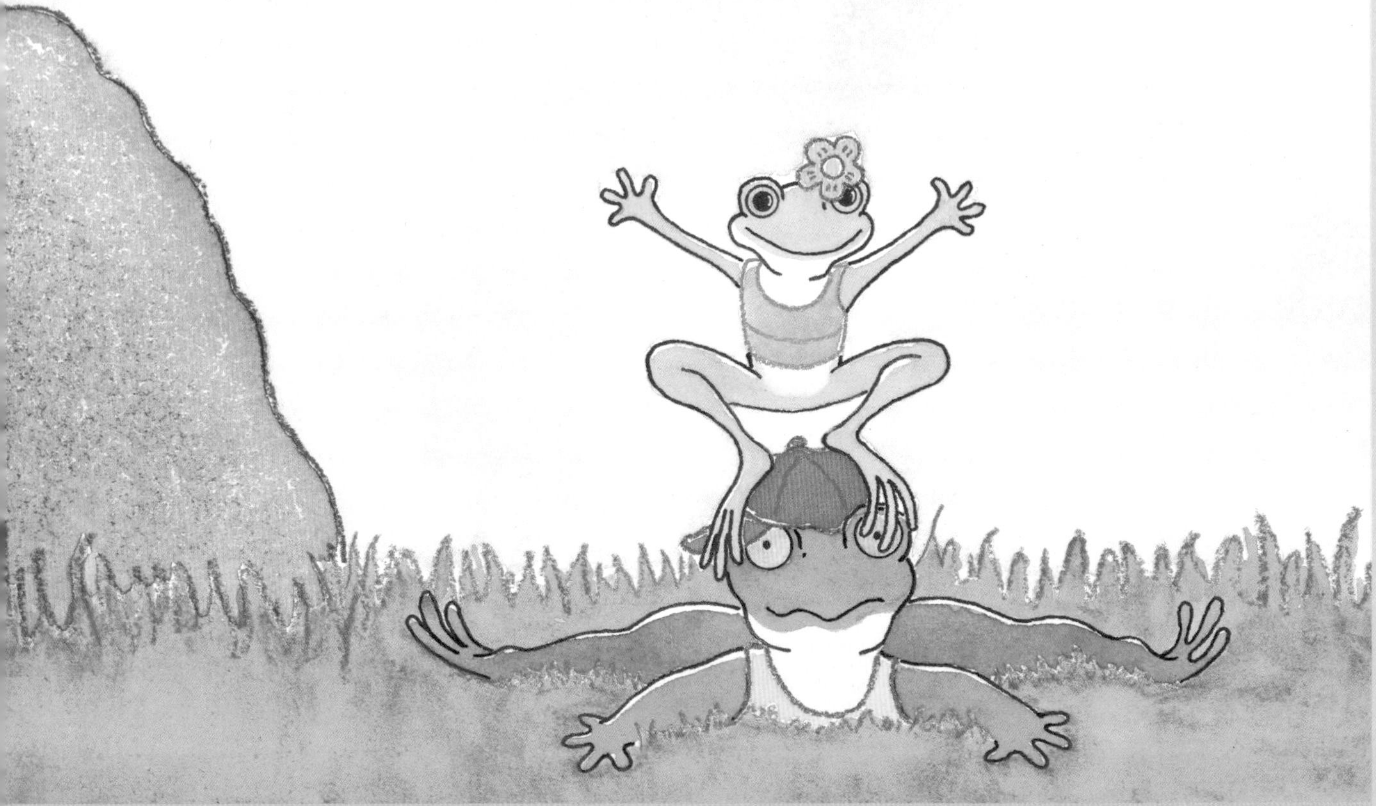

Lucy lands on Bob.